This
Naure Storybook
belongs to:

_____

_____

*For Rodney, Austin, Georgia and Nanna Thornton
whose garden was full of summertime cicadas.* LG

For our precious wildlife. JW

First published in 2019
by Walker Books Australia Pty Ltd
Locked Bag 22, Newtown
NSW 2042 Australia
www.walkerbooks.com.au

This edition published in 2022.

The moral rights of the author and illustrator have been asserted.

Text © 2019 Lesley Gibbes
Illustrations © 2019 Judy Watson

All rights reserved. No part of this publication may be reproduced, stored in a retrieval system, or transmitted in any form or by any means – electronic, mechanical, photocopying, recording or otherwise – without the prior written permission of the publisher.

 A catalogue record for this book is available from the National Library of Australia

ISBN: 978 1 760655 48 8

The illustrations for this book were created with pencil, brush and ink, and monotype and then assembled and coloured in Photoshop.

Typeset in Godlike and GFY Palmer
Printed and bound in China

1 2 3 4 5 6 7 8 9 10

SEARCHING FOR CICADAS

Lesley Gibbes and Judy Watson

WALKER BOOKS
AND SUBSIDIARIES

LONDON • BOSTON • SYDNEY • AUCKLAND

In the summertime, Grandpa and I go cicada-watching. I collect the tent and sleeping bags and Grandpa packs the cooler.

A cicada is a large flying insect. It has a stout body with six legs and 2 pairs of wings that fold over its back.

We put our camping gear into my wagon and walk down to Apex Reserve.

Last year we found five Green Grocers, three Yellow Mondays and one Floury Baker.

This year I want to see a Black Prince. Grandpa says they're as rare as hen's teeth.

The Green Grocer, Yellow Monday and Black Prince cicadas are all named after their colour. Some cicadas like the Double Drummer are named after the sound they make.

We pitch our tent and wait for the sun to set.

The cicadas are so loud I cover my ears.

Grandpa says it's the male cicada that makes all the noise. He's calling for a mate.

Certain cicada calls are loud enough to cause pain to the human ear. Others are so high-pitched their songs can't be heard by humans at all. When a male cicada sings it creases its ears so it's not deafened by its own noise. The female cicada can make sound too. If she likes a male cicada's song she will flick her wings together.

Most people search for cicadas in trees, but the real secret to finding cicadas is to look for cicada nymphs on the ground.

Our favourite spot is the wavy grass under the old grey gum.

A nymph is a baby cicada. The female cicada lays hundreds of tiny rice-shaped eggs into slits that she has cut into the branches of trees, shrubs or grasses. The eggs hatch into small wingless nymphs.

"I found one!" I say.

It's brown and soft and very ugly. I think it looks like an alien from outer space.

"It's a beauty!" says Grandpa.

I watch as my nymph climbs onto the trunk of the gum tree.

Grandpa says the nymph lives underground for years before it digs its way to the surface. Then, like magic, it changes into an adult cicada all in one night.

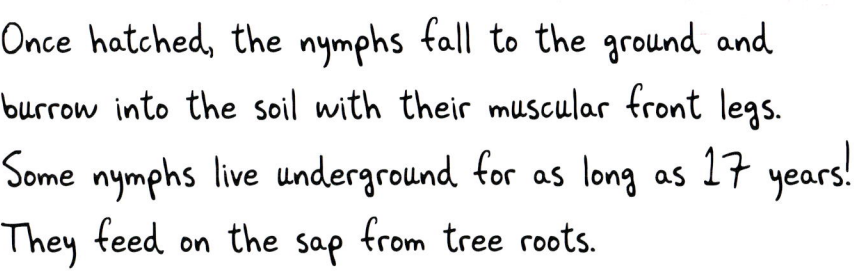

Once hatched, the nymphs fall to the ground and burrow into the soil with their muscular front legs. Some nymphs live underground for as long as 17 years! They feed on the sap from tree roots.

When the sun sets
I turn on my torch.

Now we watch
and wait.

When a nymph is fully grown it will burrow out of the soil and climb up a tree or other upright object. It sheds its outer casing and emerges as an adult cicada with wings.

"Look, Grandpa!"

One of the nymphs has split its skin. It wriggles and pushes its way out, first the head then the body with legs and wings. It's all wet and its wings are shrivelled. By morning it will be dry and the wings will be long and hard.

"Time for bed," says Grandpa.

I'm so excited it's hard to sleep.

Adult cicadas have two pairs of glassy transparent wings that are strengthened by veins. When an adult cicada emerges from its shell, its wings inflate with fluid then harden. A cicada's wings can be 2.5 cm to 15 cm long, depending on the species.

In the morning, all the nymphs have split their skins.
Their empty shells still cling to the gum tree.

The prickly legs of the empty nymph shell allow it to cling to most surfaces.

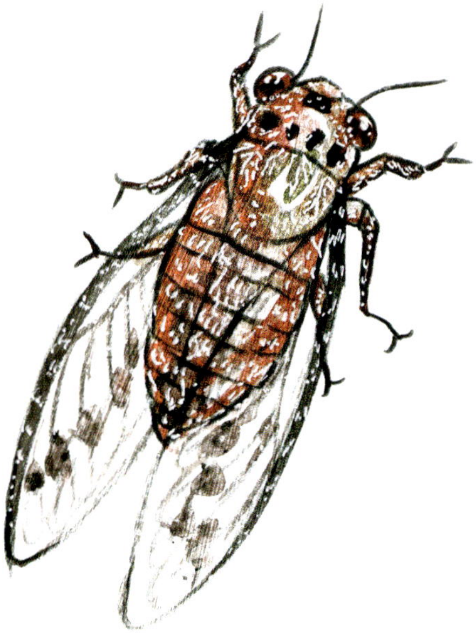

I count four Green Grocers, three Floury Bakers and two Yellow Mondays.

The Green Grocer cicada is one of the loudest cicadas in the world. The Floury Baker cicada gets its name from the flour-like dust that covers its body.

But there's one more. It's a Black Prince!

I show Grandpa. He can't believe it! He grabs his camera and takes a photo before it flies away.

Everyone will want to see our photo of the Black Prince. We'll be famous!

The Black Prince cicada is not common in city areas. It is usually found in the she-oak tree that grows on the banks of rivers.

Grandpa and I lie in the cool grass.

We watch the cicadas buzz and whizz all afternoon.

Grandpa says they only live for a few weeks and they have lots of work to do, like finding a mate and laying eggs.

Cicadas are hard to keep alive in captivity because they need to feed on flowing sap from trees. They suck the tree fluids through a straw-like mouthpart. Most adult cicadas live between 2 to 4 weeks.

When we pack up, there's one more cicada surprise.

The Black Prince lands on my hand. His wings tickle my fingers and I laugh.

Then he whirls and spins and disappears into the afternoon sun.

We're both sad to see him go.

Grandpa says if he finds a mate we might just see another Black Prince next year. I can't wait!

INFORMATION ABOUT CICADAS

Cicadas can be found on every continent except Antarctica. They are the loudest insects in the world. They don't bite or sting, however they do have prickly feet and a beak that can pinch or scratch. To tell the difference between male and female cicadas, look at the shape of their abdomen (stomach). A male cicada's abdomen is square and a female's is pointed. The best time to see cicada nymphs is at dusk. Look, but don't touch! A nymph needs plenty of room to shed its skin and dry its delicate wings. If the wings are touched before they dry they may not form properly.

ABOUT THE AUTHOR

LESLEY GIBBES grew up in Sydney's Northern Beaches and Wagga Wagga in country NSW. After completing a Bachelor of Education at the University of Sydney she embarked on a successful sixteen-year teaching career in Primary Education specialising in dance, drama, debating and public speaking. She is now a multiple-award-winning, internationally published author of books for children.

ABOUT THE ILLUSTRATOR

JUDY WATSON grew up in a house behind her father's veterinary clinic, and spent all her holidays on a farm near the beach. When she was not reading or drawing, she could be found lying in the long grass watching bugs and birds. Judy's first picture book won the Prime Minister's Literary Award for Children's Fiction. She has illustrated over 20 books for children. She particularly enjoyed drawing Australian plants for this book.

INDEX

Black Princes 9, 22, 27
calls 10, 11
colour 9, 21
Double Drummers 9
eggs 12, 25
feeding 15, 25
females 11, 12, 28
Floury Bakers 9, 21
Green Grocers 9, 21
habitat 22, 28
legs 7, 15, 18, 21
males 10, 11, 28
mates 10, 25, 27
nymphs 12, 15, 17, 18, 21, 28
shells 19, 21
sound 9, 11
trees 12, 15, 17, 21, 22, 25
wings 7, 11, 12, 17, 18, 19, 27, 28
Yellow Mondays 9, 21

Look up the pages to find out about all these cicada things.

Don't forget to look at both kinds of word – this kind and this kind.

Nature Storybooks

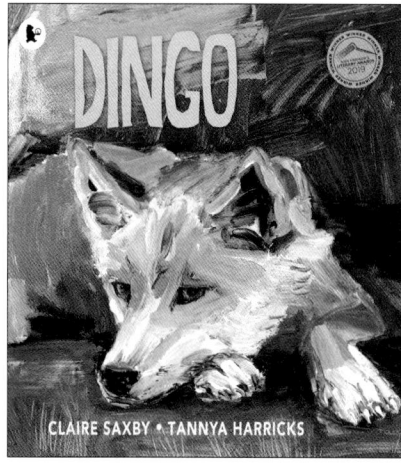

DESERT LAKE:
THE STORY OF KATI THANDA – LAKE EYRE
by Pamela Freeman
illustrated by Liz Anelli

NOTABLE BOOK, CBCA BOOK OF THE YEAR AWARDS, EVEN POWNALL AWARD FOR INFORMATION BOOKS, 2017
NOTABLE BOOK, CBCA BOOK OF THE YEAR AWARDS, PICTURE BOOKS, 2017
SHORTLISTED, NSW 2017 PREMIER'S LITERARY AWARD, THE NSW PREMIER'S HISTORY AWARDS, THE ENVIRONMENT AWARD FOR CHILDREN'S LITERATURE AND THE EDUCATIONAL PUBLISHING AWARDS

"With appealing text and visuals, this well-researched information book would make a valuable addition to any primary-school classroom intending to study Australian landscapes, climate change and the arts."
Books+Publishing

Paperback 978-1-760650-38-4

KOALA
by Claire Saxby
illustrated by Julie Vivas

HONOUR BOOK, CBCA BOOK OF THE YEAR AWARDS, EVEN POWNALL AWARD FOR INFORMATION BOOKS, 2018

"Beautifully written ... heartfelt narrative with factual information ... A gorgeous publication, Koala is sure to be another success as he finds his own way home, right into the hearts of young Australians."
Aussie Reviews

Paperback 978-1-760650-91-9

DINGO
by Claire Saxby
illustrated by Tannya Harricks

Can you see her? There – deep in the stretching shadows – a dingo. Her pointed ears twitch. Her tawny eyes flash in the low-slung sun. Dingo listens. Dusk is a busy time. Dusk is the time for hunting.

"A beautiful narrative nonfiction nature book that may well become a classic."
Reading Time magazine

Hardback 978-1-925381-28-3
Paperback 978-1-760651-56-5